WARNING!!!!

Hyperspace is a Choose Your Own Adventure®
book. Do not read it straight through from beginning to end. Instead, start at page one and read
until you come to your first choice. The adven-
tures you have will be the result of the decisions
you make. After you make your choice, follow
the instructions to see what happens to you next.

A SPECIAL NOTE
TO THE READER

Hyperspace is different even from other Choose
Your Own Adventure® books. Your journey will
not take you just to the stars or other galaxies, but
to other universes *and other realities*.

Not only will you face terrible dangers, even
the laws of science may change before your eyes!
What seems to be real may be only a story, and
what seems to be a story may be real. In
Hyperspace anything can happen. Anything.

Good wishes and good luck.

Edward Packard

SPECIAL WARNING!!!!

Many scientists think that they have some idea of the size of the universe, how long ago it came into existence, and when it might end. But no one can say whether ours is the only universe or whether there is an infinite number of universes. If there is an infinite number, then some of them may be very much like our own!

Professor Karl Zinka has devoted his life to finding out whether other universes exist outside our own time and space. You are about to be drawn into his quest. To do so you will have to enter hyperspace.

Hyperspace is so strange that it almost cannot be described in words. Some people believe that hyperspace is four-dimensional space. It may be even stranger than that. It may involve a world of

five or six or even more dimensions. Certainly the laws of science may be different there. This makes it possible to travel to another universe in an instant instead of the many hundreds of years it would take to get there by traveling through the third dimension. One thing seems certain: hyperspace is the only means by which we could reach another universe, or something in another universe could reach us.

What is it like to be in hyperspace? There are many possibilities, more than we can imagine. To get one idea of what it *might* be like, imagine that you are an ant and that you have spent your entire life inside a large balloon. The inside of that balloon is your entire universe. Suddenly the balloon bursts. At *that* moment you've entered *hyperspace*.

Are you ready to begin your adventure? I hope so, because it's about to begin.

Ever since Professor Karl Zinka moved into your neighborhood, you've been wanting to meet him. You've seen him a few times, out for a stroll, puffing on his white clay pipe—a strange-looking little man with a few stringy hairs on his head and a gray beard cut in the shape of a triangle. People say he's a mathematical genius. You wonder what he does all day.

One afternoon you have a chance to find out, for you happen to be passing his house as he is returning from his walk.

"Come in. I'm glad to meet you," he says when you introduce yourself. "I've been so busy, I haven't had time to call on my neighbors."

Shaking hands, you say, "I'm glad to meet you, too, Professor. I've been curious about your work."

The professor smiles. "My work is not easy to describe. Only a few people can understand it, but wait—I'll be right back."

The professor hurries into another room, almost tripping over his calico cat. A moment later he reappears with a book. There is a twinkle in his eye as he hands it to you. "Even if you don't understand higher mathematics, I think you'll find this interesting. Would you like to borrow it?"

You glance at the cover of the book. Its title is *Hyperspace*.

If you take the book, thank him, and leave,
turn to page 3.

If you stay and talk some more, turn to page 6.

Back at home, you prop yourself up with some cushions and start to read the book.

Imagine that you are absolutely flat, and that you live on a flat surface, you read. *You can travel backward and forward and sideways, but never up and down. In fact, you never even know there is an up and down!*

Of course in the real world you can move backward and forward AND up and down. But imagine still another way you could travel—a way we cannot even describe. If you could move in THAT way, you'd be in hyperspace.

You look up for a moment and blink. This book is a little strange. You wonder whether it's worth reading on to the next page or whether you should skip ahead a few pages and look for some real action.

If you read on to the next page, go on to page 4.

If you skip ahead, turn to page 10.

The implications of hyperspace are staggering, the book continues. *Not only are there other dimensions that we cannot perceive though they govern our destiny, but there are infinite numbers of universes, each of them as complex as our own. And traveling in hyperspace is the only way to reach them. Strangest of all, these other universes do not always lie somewhere far beyond our own. They may exist around and within us! The most important scientific question of today is this: can we enter hyperspace, can we reach another universe?*

Just then the phone rings, and you put your book aside to answer it.

"Hello. I'm glad I caught you." The voice sounds like Professor Zinka's.

"Professor, is that you?"

"Yes, and I want to warn you not to come near my house. Something's gone wrong with my experiment."

Turn to page 23.

"I don't want there to be two of me," you say. "I just want to get back to my own universe!" Your hand comes down on the red lever.

The professor shouts, "No—it's not set!"

You remember nothing after that. All you know is that now you're lying in a hospital bed with a nurse and doctor standing nearby. You wiggle your arms and legs. Except for a dull headache, you feel okay. It looks as if you made it. But the doctor appears grave.

You try to smile. "Where am I? What day is it?" You want to ask what universe you're in, but you don't want to sound crazy.

"We know all about you," the doctor says. "You want to know whether you reached your own universe."

"Yes, but how did you know—?"

Turn to page 27.

"Thanks for lending me the book," you tell the professor, "but could you just tell me a bit more about what you do?"

The professor smiles. "I'll show you my laboratory, but don't expect to understand much." He leads you through a dark, musty library. The walls are lined with bookcases that reach the ceiling. More books are stacked in huge piles on the floor.

The professor opens another door, and you follow him into a small room with perfectly round walls. The entire roof is a transparent dome. In the center of the room, resting on a pedestal, is a stainless steel globe about the size of a basketball. Just below it is a panel on which are mounted a red lever and a green lever. Computer consoles and rows of steel cabinets, faced with electronic display screens, line the walls.

"What's that?" you ask, pointing to the globe.

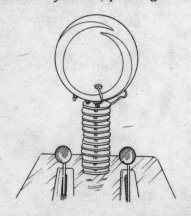

Turn to page 15.

You hate to do it, but it's self-defense. Pft! Pft! Pft! Your laser-driven impulse cannon selects its targets. You obliterate the enemy craft one by one!

You're thankful to have survived—your astrocraft must have a very advanced design. At the same time, you feel sick at having destroyed other spacecraft and their pilots.

How strange that they didn't burst into flames or crash! They just disappeared. And now something even stranger is happening. A lush meadow is visible below, and your spacecraft is gently descending toward it as if guided by an unseen hand.

Moments later your craft lands—so precisely that it takes you a minute to realize it has come to rest. Warily you open the canopy and step out. Three other spacecraft rest nearby. They look like the ones you shot down—or, rather, the ones that disappeared when you shot at them. You have an eerie feeling that somehow they are the very same craft!

Turn to page 46.

"Science must go on, Professor," you say.

The professor gravely lays a hand on your shoulder. "You have courage, and you have given me courage. I must act before I change my mind."

You start to worry about what might happen if something goes wrong, but it is already too late. The professor pushes down on the red lever.

You feel an electric charge in the air. The professor's face freezes in the beginning of a smile. You can't move a muscle. A loud, pulsating hum is coming from the steel globe. It rises in pitch until your ears are assailed by an electronic chord of incredible magnitude. The professor dives to the floor. You try to do the same, but it's no use—you might as well be encased in ice. An instant later you black out.

Turn to page 20.

"Maybe you should consult with other scientists and see what they say," you suggest.

The professor is shaking as he rests his hand on a red lever. "No. I am certain this machine will work, because it does not depend on mechanical parts but on mathematics."

"But—"

Too late. The professor has pulled the lever and *vanished*.

The machine must have worked! The professor wouldn't have disappeared unless he had entered hyperspace. That in itself is a remarkable achievement. Whether he made it to another universe is another question.

You feel an irresistible urge to follow. It's risky, but your taste for adventure is very strong.

If you yield to the urge and pull the red lever, turn to page 26.

If you avoid touching any of the controls, turn to page 29.

If you pull the green lever hoping it will reverse the process and bring the professor back, turn to page 33.

10

It was a good idea to turn to this page. You can tell you're in for plenty of action. And, much to your surprise, the page is set up like a Choose Your Own Adventure® book!

Imagine that your spacecraft has just entered hyperspace, you read. You streak through a black hole and instantly enter another universe. You're in a new state of existence where even the laws of physics are different!

Suddenly three disc-shaped craft close in on you. They must take you to be an intruder. Quickly you activate the radio and shout into the transceiver, "Don't fire! I come in friendship!"

Turn to page 14.

"Obviously," says the professor, "he didn't make it." He pauses a moment. "Unless . . . it was *I* who didn't make it, and we're still here, and it's one of *you* who came from the other universe!"

"So how can we tell which of us is from the other universe?" you ask.

The professor pulls at his triangular beard. "You should go outside and look around for differences. To one of you things will look exactly the same. The other will notice that some things are different, because it's unlikely that the two universes are *exactly* the same."

"Do you want to come with me?" asks the other you.

You're confused. Is this really happening, or is the professor playing a trick on you? Maybe he's hypnotized you!

If you decide to go exploring with the other you, turn to page 56.

If you decide that you're in another universe, and that you should reactivate the hypolaser and try to get back to your own universe, turn to page 5.

If you decide that you're still in your own universe and that you'll just walk out and go home, turn to page 24.

There is a terrible urgency in the professor's voice, and you lunge at the lever. Instantly you are paralyzed by an electric charge that floods the room with quivering light. The two of you crumple to the floor. You feel as if every ounce of strength has been drained from your body.

Finally the burst of electricity dies away and the eerie light fades. Several minutes pass before the professor is able to pull himself together and inspect his instruments. Then he walks over and helps you to your feet. "We stopped it! We sealed the hole to a hostile universe! If you hadn't come when you did, it would have been all over—not only for us, but for the earth, and even for our universe!"

You hardly know what to believe. Is the professor a genius or is he crazy? "I think I'd better get home now," you say, "or I'll be late for dinner."

"I'm grateful for your help," the professor says. He shakes your hand again and again. "More grateful than I can say. Someday I will repay you for what you've done."

Turn to page 35.

You hear unintelligible squawks in reply. No chance for communication—they're not human. They must think you're a space invader, and there's no way you can tell them you're friendly. You've got to act fast!

If you open fire, turn to page 7.

If you hold your fire and try to maneuver safely past the oncoming craft, turn to page 18.

If you reverse your course and try to go back through the black hole, turn to page 19.

"The hypolaser—a device capable of focusing light photons into a geometric point!" Professor Zinka stares at you intently. "Do you know how small a geometric point is? Like the point where two sides of a triangle meet?"

"Very small, I guess."

"Not just *very* small," says the professor. His eyes shine with excitement. "*Infinitely* small. Think about this: if you could focus a light on an infinitely small point, its brightness at that point would be infinite!"

"What would happen then?"

"You would penetrate hyperspace. You might puncture a hole in the skin that separates us from another universe."

"Then what?"

The professor shakes his head. "I don't know. But the hypolaser is designed to answer that question. It's been ready for over a month, but I haven't had the courage to activate it. You see, I can't be entirely sure what will happen."

"Do you think you'll ever try it?"

The professor points his unlit pipe at you. "My whole life's work has been devoted to this. It would be unthinkable to turn back now. Still, I must confess I feel as if I'm about to jump off a cliff."

If you urge Professor Zinka to activate the hypolaser, turn to page 8.

If you advise him not to risk it, turn to page 9.

"Police Headquarters," a brisk voice answers.

"Officer, my neighbor Professor Zinka just called. He said something was wrong. Then I think the phone went dead."

You give the address and wait outside. It's only a few minutes before a squad car pulls up and two policemen get out. You are leading them toward the professor's door when he comes stumbling out of the house.

"Professor!" You run toward him. "Are you all right?"

He shakes his head. "None of us is all right! The hole I punctured has connected us to a hostile universe. I tried to stop the flow but . . . *too late.*"

One of the officers steps forward and takes the professor gently by the arm. "I think you've been working too hard, Professor."

"Why don't you come along with us to the hospital?" the other policeman adds. "Maybe you ought to check in for a few days."

It does seem as if the professor has lost his mind. But something about his face tells you he's not crazy.

"Just a moment," you say to the officers. "Professor, what do you mean by a flow from a hostile universe?"

"Look!" He points toward his house. You stand there open-mouthed, trying not to believe your eyes. The professor's house is silently crumbling into a pile of ashes!

Turn to page 51.

18

You try to maneuver past the oncoming missiles, pulling down on one lever and then another, desperately trying to master the intricate controls. Your craft plummets, swerves, and climbs at sickening rates. You feel sure you'll be shot down. Even if you escape the oncoming missiles, you'll crack up. You don't really know how to fly this craft.

Turn to page 32.

Swiftly you swing the directional lever hard over and brace yourself. The spacecraft swerves in a tight arc and then accelerates toward the black hole. The enemy craft drop into formation behind you, but you rapidly pull away.

Now you need only concern yourself with the black hole. Just because you made it through once doesn't mean you'll make it this time. The normal laws of physics do not apply inside a black hole. The odds are always against you.

You hurtle toward the abyss at ever-increasing speed. Thickening clusters of stars seem to surround you, their light rays bent by extreme gravity.

Your instruments show that your craft is approaching the speed of light. Soon your fate will be sealed. You wish it were over with. Why is it taking so long? You glance at your watch, then at the ship's chronometer. Something is wrong. Time seems frozen. Vaguely you remember something about relativity theory—time slows as an object approaches the speed of light.

Suddenly it dawns on you: time is slowing to a complete stop. You will be spared from being torn apart in the black hole, because you will never reach it. You will never even reach the end of this book . . . .

Turn to page 112.

Slowly you come to. All is calm, and you can move about freely. You look dazedly around the room. Like you, the professor is lying on the floor; he's unconscious but still breathing. Both of you must have been knocked out. Now that the danger is past, though, you regret not actually reaching hyperspace.

"Where did you come from?" The voice behind you sounds strangely like your own. Turning, you're astonished to see someone who looks exactly like you!

"Where did *you* come from?" you answer.

"It worked! I did it!" The professor leaps to his feet.

"What do you mean?" you ask.

"You've crossed into another universe! Or . . ." he points to your double, "*you* have!"

"How could that be?" you demand. "It *looks* like our universe, except for this kid who looks like me."

"Yes, how could it be?" asks the other you.

"It's not surprising." The professor is flushed with excitement. "If, as I predicted, there is an infinite number of universes, then there must be some that correspond almost exactly to our own—even in such details as having a professor like me and a kid like you. This phenomenon would occur in a *parallel* universe."

"Then where is the other professor?" asks the other you.

Turn to page 11.

You run to the professor's house and throw open the front door.

"Professor!" you call. "Are you all right?" Hearing a muffled voice from within, you rush through the house and find the professor in his laboratory, working feverishly at his computer.

He glances at you for an instant. "Hyperspace is leaking in! I'm trying to block it—trying to plug the hole that separates us from an alien universe. Quick, throw the green lever to the left of the door!"

Turn to page 13.

"What happened?" you ask.

"I thought I would be able to enter hyperspace. Instead, my molecular structure has started to break down. It's as if hyperspace has entered me!"

There is a click at the other end of the phone, leaving you surprised and uneasy. You wonder if you should go to the professor's house and see whether he's all right or if you ought to call the police.

If you run to the professor's house and knock on his door, turn to page 22.

If you call the police, turn to page 16.

"No thanks," you say. "I just can't believe we've traveled to another universe. I'm going home." You throw open the door and start through the professor's library.

"Be careful!" he calls after you. "If this *is* another universe, some things may be different than in ours. That could be dangerous!"

With the professor's words ringing in your ears, you fling open the front door and run down the street toward home. Everything looks just the same. But as you walk down the path toward your house, you stop short. Your dog is waiting to

Go on to the next page.

meet you, his tail wagging—but there's something strange about him. He has green eyes instead of brown, and long whiskers like a big cat. You open the front door of your house. Now you're fearful of what else may be changed.

"Hi! It's almost time for dinner!"

Thank goodness! Mom's home, and she's *your* mom. You've never been so glad to see her, even though she's frowning.

"It's about time you got home," she says. "You still have a lot of packing to do!"

"Packing?"

She laughs. "Come on, silly—you know we're moving to Moropa tomorrow! Six A.M. and we're out of this house!"

"Moving? Moropa?" Your face falls.

"What's the matter, dear?" she asks.

"Mom, I've forgotten—just where is Moropa?"

"Why, you know—it's just across the Paclantic Sea."

Paclantic Sea? This can't be earth. That can't be *Mom.* You must be in another universe!

Turn to page 28.

You pull down on the red lever. In an instant you can neither see, hear, taste, smell, nor feel anything!

Somehow the hypolaser failed to connect you with another universe. Instead you're drifting into hyperspace, and you're in a mode of hyperspace where you have no sensory impressions at all. It's as if you were floating in a tank of warm water in a dark, soundproof chamber where you don't even have to breathe!

You feel oddly relaxed, even though you should be scared. You like it—or, rather, you would like it, if you didn't have to think about what could happen next. You might die instantly, or you might drift like this forever. What's worse is that you have no control over your fate—nothing to decide, nothing to do.

Turn to page 37.

The doctor stops you with an upraised hand. "You've traveled through hyperspace, but your trip was incomplete. You did not reach a *real* universe, but an imaginary one!"

"What do you mean?"

The nurse gently takes your hand. "I know it's hard to accept, but the problem is that . . . *you're not real now.*"

"You're only imaginary," the doctor adds, "like a character in a book or a figure in a painting. In your case, you're only a person in a dream, like the nurse and me here."

"We're only existing in a dream?" You feel stunned. The idea seems even stranger than passing into another universe. Is the doctor playing a cruel joke on you? Certainly no real doctor would do that, at least not in *your* universe. A chill sweeps over you.

Turn to page 31.

The only thing to do now is to go back to the professor's house and see if he can transport you back to your own universe. But, much as you want to get home, you're not confident that the professor can get you there. You might end up in a much worse universe than the one you're in now.

If you run to Professor Zinka's house in hopes of getting back to your own universe, turn to page 63.

If you just play along with your new "Mom," turn to page 64.

You step back and stand quietly, hoping the professor will return. After an hour's wait, you walk sadly back home, troubled with questions about his fate. How foolish he was to fling himself into a void of mystery! Still, you have to admire him. He must be a genius if he's actually invented a way to reach hyperspace. To be able to return, though—that would take a supergenius!

Turn to page 38.

"Do you mean that when the person having the dream wakes up, we'll die?" you ask.

"Well, I wouldn't put it that way," answers the doctor. "After all, if you're only imaginary, there's no way you can die, because you aren't really alive."

"Doctor, can't we postpone the operation?" The words come from an elderly man lying in the bed next to yours.

The doctor bends over him. "I'm afraid not, Mr. Gravly."

The nurse leans toward you and says, "That man—in the bed—*he's* the one having the dream. We only exist in his dream. It's a nightmare, in fact. He's dreaming that he's about to have a serious operation."

You watch helplessly as the doctor listens to the old man's heartbeat through his stethoscope. "It's time to take him to the operating room," the doctor says.

At that moment an orderly enters the room. He wheels Mr. Gravly's bed toward the door. Suddenly you realize that when Mr. Gravly leaves the room, he'll probably stop dreaming about you. Then you won't even exist in his dream, much less in real life.

If you try to follow Mr. Gravly so as to make sure you'll still be in the dream, turn to page 89.

If you feel it's hopeless to do anything and you might as well lie back and accept your fate, turn to page 59.

But to your amazement, your machine dives, climbs, banks, and rolls as if you were an ace. How can this be happening? The computer must be programmed to compensate for your errors and keep the craft flying no matter what you do!

Suddenly a missile explodes only a few hundred meters ahead. Traveling at a thousand times the speed of sound, your craft will reach the deadly sphere of radiating heat and light almost instantly. You have only a fraction of a second—time for one thought—before the world goes blank.

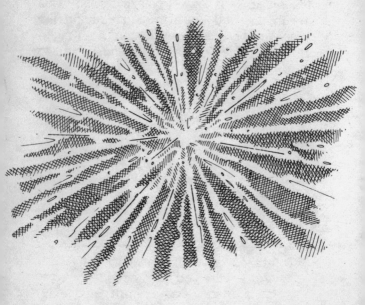

Turn to page 53.

Hoping you can bring the professor back, you pull down the green lever. Nothing happens. The more you think about it, the more you realize that your chances of making it safely to another universe are slim. Even the professor, with all of his mathematical knowledge, is unlikely to return.

The minutes tick away. You begin to lose hope. You wait a little longer and then head for home. But you barely reach the street before you hear an explosion behind you.

Turn to page 41.

Several months go by without any sign of the professor. You often wonder where he is and what he's up to. You miss seeing him strolling along on his walk. On the other hand, his experiments were pretty scary, and, in a way, you're glad that he's gone.

Still, you are delighted when a large package wrapped in heavy brown paper arrives in the mail. The return address reads:

> Professor Karl Zinka
> Spica Laboratories
> Kartoom, Alberta, Canada

Eagerly you rip open the envelope pasted on the box. As you'd guessed, it's a letter from the professor!

Turn to page 42.

"No, but . . ."

And he is gone.

You stand there alone and puzzled. What would the professor have said after the word "but"? You feel that the whole mystery of the universe lies beyond that word.

The End

You hate it. Hate! Well, at least you have an emotion. Hyperspace has not destroyed your spirit.

Can emotion affect destiny? Perhaps it can—at least in hyperspace. For some reason you feel certain that, as long as you have hope, you have a chance. And suddenly you realize that you not only have a chance; you have a choice. It is a staggering choice, with very few clues. You are trapped in the fourth dimension of hyperspace: a world or condition in which you cannot control your destiny. Yet you sense that you have one power—*the power to will yourself either forward into the fifth dimension or back into the third-dimensional world from which you came.*

If you will yourself forward into the fifth dimension, turn to page 66.

If you will yourself back into the three-dimensional world from which you came, turn to page 65.

One day, weeks later, you are astonished to answer the phone and hear the professor's voice.

"Is it really *you?*" you shout into the phone.

"Please come right over!" he says. *"Hurry!"*

You rush to the professor's house and are glad to find him seated in his study puffing on his pipe as if nothing had happened.

"We have only a couple of minutes to talk," he says. "Then I must return to my new universe. The hypolaser worked, but only because of a fortunate alignment between this universe and the one where I've chosen to exist. I'll call it Universe X."

Turn to page 50.

You rush back, fearing the worst. Cautiously you open the front door. The house smells like a burnt-out electrical circuit. You pause at the door to the laboratory, fearful of what may lie behind it. But you've come this far; you'd be cowardly to turn back now. As you touch the door, it falls over with a crash. Its hinges have melted off. The hypolaser is disintegrating into dust.

Miraculously, Professor Zinka is still alive! Lying on the floor, his suit torn and covered with dust, he mumbles words you can't understand.

"Professor, are you all right?"

Slowly he pulls himself to his feet, staring at you dumbly as if he doesn't understand you.

"Are you all right?" you ask once more.

He shakes his head again and again. Finally he mumbles, "I never thought I'd make it back."

"Too bad your equipment is ruined," you say.

The professor hobbles a few steps toward you. "It's just as well. I wouldn't want to use it again. What I went through was too horrible to describe. I can tell you this: our universe is far from perfect, but I never want to leave it again."

The End

Kartoom, Alberta

To my old young friend:

I've settled here permanently and will not be returning to the United States for a long time. But I haven't forgotten to repay you for what you did. Inside this box is a small round bottle made of an unbreakable glass of my own design. The bottle has a cap that will open if you turn it fourteen times.

Its contents could be worth a fortune.

Do you remember when we sealed off the hole and stopped the leakage of hyperspace into our universe? After you left, I realized that some hyperspace (specifically, a gaseous substance subject to the laws of gravity of another universe) had gotten into the laboratory.

Go on to the next page.

Using a polarizing diffractor I was able to trap it in two bottles. I have kept one. The other is in the box you hold. If the bottle is opened and hyperspace is allowed to mix with the air, the laws of gravity in the vicinity of the bottle will be radically altered. By holding on to the bottle you could become weightless. You would rise above the tree-tops and drift across the countryside as if you were riding in a balloon. Gradually the hyperspace would evaporate and you would drift to the ground.

This bottle can only be used once. Since its effects may be dangerous, I suggest that you save it for a very special occasion.

Sincerely,
Professor Karl Zinka

Turn to page 68.

"Car Fourteen. We have a serious emergency!" The other cop is on the radio.

"Yes, it's spreading," says the professor, "and there's no way to stop it. There is no cohesion of matter in the universe that is leaking into ours. *We* take it for granted that things hold together, but the alien laws of a formless and shapeless universe are overwhelming us. The nuclear force that holds molecules together is going—"

"Look at that car! It just turned into dust!" The officer at the wheel seems paralyzed with fear.

The other policeman grabs him by the shoulder. "We've got to block off this area!"

"It's no use," says the professor. His voice is hollow. "There's no way of stopping it. Even if we could get to the moon, it wouldn't help. Our entire universe is doomed."

The driver seems hypnotized by the sight of houses, cars, and trees silently turning to dust. Suddenly a gust of wind sweeps the dust up into a whirling gray cloud.

"Step on the gas!" you cry. "We've got to get out of . . ."

The End

The alien pilots are standing nearby. Vaguely humanlike, covered with short, sleek hair, they smile and wave their spindly arms.

One of them steps forward. He bows as if you were a welcome hero! In his hands is a shiny black object shaped like a clam. It emits a loud musical tone as a computer voice speaks: "Congratulations! You have won the battle; you have conquered our kingdom. You will be ruler of our world!"

Turn to page 54.

"Help, I'll fall!" you scream.

Your new friends laugh. "Don't worry," Telar says, as you all float upward. "We control gravity with thought waves."

"I don't want to brag," Raza comments, "but there are only a few universes where you can do that."

"Wow," you say, "this is some place!"

"You've hardly seen anything yet," says Telar, as the three of you float gently back to the ground. "But you are a free creature and not a captive. Do you want to stay, or would you rather go home?"

If you decide to stay, turn to page 70.

If you say you'd rather go home, turn to page 72.

The aliens scowl and shake their heads. One of them steps forward and points a long, thin finger at you. His stern, round eyes burn into yours, and his voice is cold as steel. He seizes the computer from his comrade and thrusts it toward you. You start to speak but are silenced by the loud musical tone and then by these words: "You defeated our patrol ships. You showed yourself to be a conqueror. Justice requires that you will be our ruler."

"No, please!" you shout.

But the aliens have already placed a heavy gold crown upon your head.

The End

Turn to page 112.

You start to ask a question, but the professor holds up a hand. "Please, there's no time for questions. I have very little time. The alignment necessary for travel through hyperspace will only last ninety more seconds. After that, this equipment will be useless. It will be scrapped as the product of a deranged mind. Scientists will pore over my mathematical formulas with interest—and maybe respect—but finally they'll scowl and dismiss them. In a sense they'll be right. I am the only scientist alive who is able to penetrate the mathematical mysteries of hyperspace."

"Just one question," you interrupt. "Why do you prefer to live in Universe X instead of this one?"

"Because I believe that Universe X is what our universe was *meant* to be. There, everything you wish were true *is* true. I have only half a minute left, so I must say goodbye and good luck!"

You're puzzled by what the professor means. "If we can never again enter hyperspace from earth, is it possible that hyperspace could come here?" you ask.

You stop yourself abruptly, knowing that the professor has only a few seconds left to answer.

Turn to page 36.

"Let's get out of here!" One of the policemen pushes you ahead of him toward the squad car.

"Come on, Professor!" You dive into the car. One of the officers shoves the professor in next to you. The other starts the engine. Then you turn and gasp as you watch trees, bushes, and another house dissolve into dust.

"I can't believe it!" cries the driver. "And it's spreading!"

Turn to page 45.

You're alive! What's more, you've never felt better. Nearby are two alien creatures—humanoid, with strange saclike pouches on each side of their long, thin necks. From their friendly expressions, you imagine that somehow they rescued you—but then why did they shoot you down?

As if he had read your mind, one of the creatures says, "My name is Telar. My friend here is Raza. You are in the Omega universe. Your brain transmits your language directly to my brain. Know that we sent you a loving greeting. When you tried to avoid it, we knew that you came from another universe where laws work differently, so we brought you safely to our planet."

"I'm grateful for your kindness," you say, "but I still don't understand."

"We must warn you," says Telar. "The laws of our universe are different from those of yours."

"How?"

Raza smiles. "Have you noticed that none of us breathes, nor do you now?"

"My gosh!" you reply. "It's true!"

"Respiration—breathing—is a primitive nuisance," says Telar. "It's quite unnecessary in any advanced universe. And have you noticed—we're not talking!"

"Oh, yes," you say, or rather think, because for the first time you notice that you've been communicating in thought waves!

"Talk, too, is very primitive," Telar says, using mental telepathy.

Suddenly you and the aliens begin to rise in the air!

Turn to page 48.

Perhaps you should feel great upon hearing these words, but instead you feel sad. You hardly make an effort to speak as the aliens lift you on their shoulders and carry you across a field to an ivory courtyard beyond which lies a marble hall. Silently they take you inside the cool, cavernous building and set you upon a gold and silver throne.

It's all so astonishing that you can't think straight. "What do you mean, I'm ruler of this world?" you finally ask.

"What it would mean in any universe," the tiny computer replies. "First of all, you must stay in this marble palace. Each day you must shake hands with visiting lords and talk with them about nothing. You must never go out without twelve guards to protect you. You must travel only in long black cars and you must never drive one yourself. You must pretend to be happy. You must always—"

"I don't WANT to be ruler!" you interrupt.

Turn to page 49.

The two of you talk and talk, but you can't make up your mind, nor can the other you. In fact, you're still discussing the situation when the professor calls to say that the time of cosmic alignment has passed. You have lost your only chance to return to your own universe. You live on, though—and very happily—on the other earth, in the other universe, with the other you.

The End

You walk out the door with the other you, sure that the two of you will become good friends. After all, you are exactly alike; you even have the same name!

Everything seems the same as it was back home except for one thing: the sky is *green!*

"I'm afraid we're in *your* universe," you say.

"Maybe you'll know better when we get home," your double replies.

The other you shows you the way home (the same way you've always gone home). You find that the house looks exactly like your own, so you move in with the family of the other you—which is also just like your own. In time they get used to having identical twins, and soon you find life very much the way it used to be.

One day you get a phone call from Professor Zinka. "Our universes will be in cosmic alignment only three hours from now," he says. "If you wish, I can return you to your own universe. Just come to my laboratory at least a half hour ahead of time so I can adjust the equipment."

Turn to page 60.

This all seems like madness. It can hardly matter what you do, so you lie back in bed and try to relax. In a moment the others leave. Now you're alone. Maybe you're only imaginary, as the doctor said, but you still seem to exist.

Your problems aren't over, though: you still don't know where you are. In fact, you don't even know which universe you're in! Maybe you should get up and do something. You jump out of bed, grateful that you still have all your clothes on, and walk briskly down the corridor. You head for the elevator. In a few minutes you'll be out of this place!

A woman is walking toward you from the nurses' station. Noticing you, she quickens her pace. Her arms are stretched toward you. She looks familiar, but you don't think you've actually met. You've only seen her picture. Perhaps it was a drawing in a book.

"I've been looking for you," the woman calls. "I heard you had been admitted to this hospital for observation."

Her voice and manner are reassuring. You trust her instinctively, and besides, she is familiar.

"I'm glad to see you," you say. "Have we met before?"

She laughs. "I think we have, if you're the person I think you are. Nera's my name—Dr. Nera Vivaldi."

Turn to page 107.

60

You run to tell the other you what the professor has said. "I want to go back, and yet I want to stay here," you say. "What do you think I should do?"

"I'm torn between those choices, too," answers the other you. "I would hate to have you leave. On the other hand, I don't want you to lose your only chance of returning to your own universe."

"What would you do if you were I?" you ask.

"I'd ask *you* to decide."

"Then decide for me."

"I'd decide to stay, if that's what you'd decide, if you were me," says the other you.

Turn to page 55.

"Peace be with you, my child." The woman's voice is soft.

"What . . . where am I? Are you a real person?" you wonder aloud. "If so, how can I see through you?"

Gesturing at the landscape around you, she says, "You've come to the far reaches of hyperspace—the fifth dimension! Here, anything can happen, things even stranger than in a book."

"You mean like in a dream?"

The woman smiles faintly. "Stranger than in a dream. *Look!*"

Turn to page 79.

As you run back to the professor's house, you notice other strange things. Some of the cars have license plates that read Texarkansas or Manitona. Along the road are long-stemmed orange flowers as big as dinner plates; you've never seen anything like them. The maple tree that used to be on the corner of your street in your universe is gone. In its place is a clump of pine trees, their needles shaped like corkscrews. You realize that the longer you stay in this universe the more differences you'll find from your own.

These little changes are maddening. Never have you wanted so much to get home! You run up to the professor's door. Without bothering to knock, you rush inside and throw open the door to the laboratory. It's empty. There's no sign of the professor or the other you. They must have entered hyperspace.

You're determined to get back to your own universe at any cost. You bring your hand down on the red lever.

Turn to page 76.

Deciding to play along, you run upstairs. "I'll pack fast, Mom," you call.

Fortunately your room is pretty much as you left it. Only a few things are peculiar, but they are *very* peculiar. There's a clock on the wall that is numbered one to fourteen. When you glance out the window, you see several stars in the sky even though it's broad daylight.

Suddenly you hear your new mom's voice. She sounds angry. "Why did you go out again, just when you promised to start packing?"

You start toward the door. Why is your new mom yelling at you? Suddenly you realize what's happened. The other you—the you that your new mom thinks *you* are—has returned.

Turn to page 77.

You close your eyes and think of the world you know. Instantly you feel as if you were being shot from a cannon. A great wind rushes past. But something is wrong. Something is terribly wrong.

For some reason your transposition was imperfect; your chromosomes were radically distorted in hyperspace. You are returning to your world, but not as yourself, or even as another human being. Life from now on will be very different, because . . .

Turn to page 84.

It's better to go forward than backward, you think, and in a fraction of a microsecond you are in *advanced* hyperspace—*the fifth dimension!*

At first, a five-dimensional world seems much like a three-dimensional world. You have command of your senses again; in fact, you see that you're standing on solid ground—gently rolling fields of hard clay colored in subtle shades of deep red and yellow brown. You start walking up a hill in order to get a better view. Soon you notice that as you climb, the ground sinks with each step so that you never get higher than you were to begin with! You try and fail again and again to get to higher ground, and you begin to panic. But you keep walking and try to stay calm.

Then you see a figure in the distance—an old woman dressed in a long robe. She is walking toward you. Her skin is pale as water and her shoulders are stooped, but her face is beautiful and she walks with the grace of a dancer. As you stare, you realize that you can see right through her, as if you were looking at a double exposure.

Turn to page 61.

You waste no time in opening the box and tossing layer after layer of plastic bubble wrap on the floor until you find the small, round bottle.

You stare at it for a long time, but of course there's not much to see. It's baffling. How can you be sure the bottle contains anything but air?

When you're ready to use it, you may find that it's a fraud. Or, from what you know of Professor Zinka, it might be even more powerful than the letter says. Instead of lifting you gently over the treetops, it could carry you up to the stratosphere, where you'd die from lack of oxygen.

What should you do with a bottle of hyperspace?

If you open it just to prove to yourself that there is really nothing in the bottle, turn to page 81.

If you decide to save it, turn to page 88.

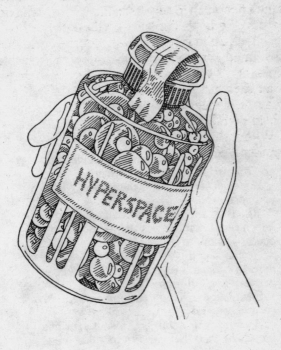

"This is pretty wild," you say. "I'll stay!"

"Very good," says Telar. "Let's go swimming."

"Great. Do you have a swimming pool?"

"Why a pool? We'll go in the ocean," says Raza.

"It might be too rough for me."

"Not under the surface!" Telar laughs.

"But I can't stay under the surface!" you protest.

"Of course you can," says Raza. "Remember that in this universe you don't need to breathe!"

"Wow, I forgot. But is the water warm enough?"

"Actually, it's very cold," says Telar, "but don't worry. Here, cold feels warm!"

You swallow hard and then ask, "Where is your ocean?"

"Right up there!" Raza points upward. "We haven't told you the best thing about our ocean—it's in the sky!"

"In the sky? Even after all I've seen, that's hard to believe," you say. "How could it possibly stay up there?"

Raza laughs. "Don't you remember? We can control gravity!"

Shaking your head, you follow your new friends as they float up into the blue green ocean in the sky.

The swimming is the best it could ever be. Soon you're sure that you'll never want to leave the Omega universe, where life is just one miracle after another.

- The End

Turn to page 112.

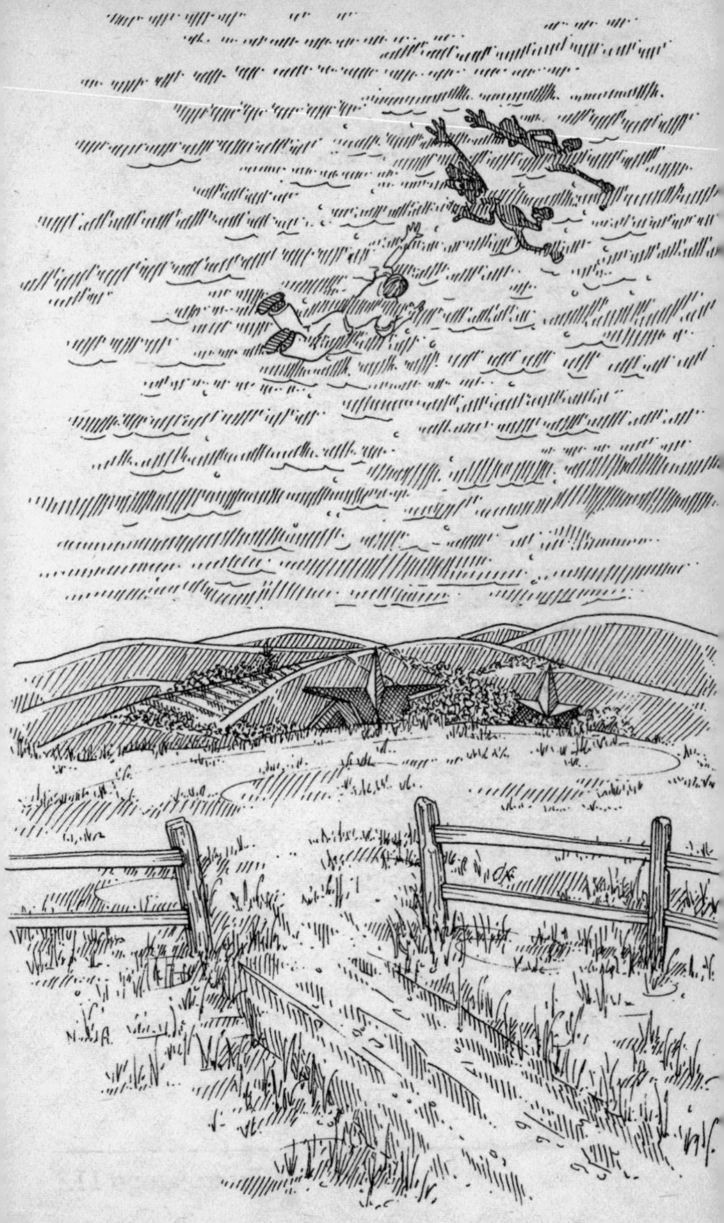

"This is all great," you say, "but things are so different. I don't think I'd ever get used to life here. Besides, I miss the folks back home."

"We quite understand," says Raza. "Then let us say goodbye."

Telar adds, "We shall never forget you!"

In a flash you've left the Omega universe . . . and you stop to think. Could the Omega universe really exist? Or could it only exist in the minds of the author and the readers of a book?

Turn to page 112.

You decide to play it cool and just make up a name. The kids throw you the Frisbee a couple of times; then Susan calls, "We've got to go home. 'Bye."

She and her brother disappear around the bend in the road. You flop down on the grass, trying to remember who and where you are. What can you do? You'd give anything to escape from this predicament, but there is no escape. You can't escape reality.

Absentmindedly you reach into your back pocket and pull out a paperback book. You must have had it with you when you lost your memory. Maybe it can give you some clue about yourself and your past life.

The title of the book is *Hyperspace,* by Professor Karl Zinka. Kind of a weird title—it must be science fiction or something. You've got nothing to lose, so you open it and riffle through a few pages, skipping a few until you come to page 10. You begin to read, and, as you read, your memory slowly returns. You realize that you're back in your own universe and that you're holding a book about the adventure you've just had.

Turn to page 10.

"All right, I'll go along," you say, "but it's not much fun being a character in a book. You don't have control over things!"

"Well, you're not as badly off as I am," says Dr. Vivaldi. "I have to do what the author tells me, but *you* are the main character. At least you get to make a decision every page or two."

"Just the same," you reply, as you follow Dr. Vivaldi out of the hospital, "it's not as good as real life."

"I suppose not, but sometimes pretty good things happen in these books. . . . *Watch out!*"

Dr. Vivaldi is pointing upward. You gasp. Scores of gleaming disc-shaped objects are filling the sky. They swoop toward you like a flock of monstrous birds.

Turn to page 82.

You walk along, trying to think. It's a strange situation. If Dr. Vivaldi is right, you'll soon come to a place where you'll have to make a choice. What will it be? How could you have become a character in a book?

Presently you come to a wire fence. Every few feet along the fence there are signs posted that say,

You could scale the fence, but you have no chance to try, for you are suddenly struck on the head from behind with a heavy, blunt object!

Turn to page 91.

Your head hurts. You're sitting on the grass in a park. People are strolling along a nearby path that curves around a small pond. Some children are feeding bread crumbs to the ducks. The scene looks vaguely familiar, though you can't remember precisely whether you've been here before. In fact, you can't precisely remember *anything*, not even who you are!

You jump to your feet, panicked. "Excuse me," you ask a woman passing by, "can you tell me where we are?"

"Why, in the park, of course," she says with a surprised look. She continues on her way.

You look around for other help. A couple of kids are playing Frisbee. Suddenly the Frisbee flies in your direction. You leap toward it and grab it out of the air.

"Nice catch. I'm Susan. Who are you?"

You gape at the girl who threw the Frisbee, wishing you could remember who you are. You've got to say *something*.

If you just make up a name, turn to page 73.

If you tell Susan that you can't remember anything and that you need help, turn to page 101.

You listen from your bedroom doorway for a few moments while the other you tries to explain the situation to your mom. Then you start toward the kitchen. Not surprisingly, Mom is upset to find out that she suddenly has twins.

Soon your dad comes home. You're glad to see that he, too, seems to be the same as the one you left behind. Like your mom, he can't seem to tell you from the other you.

At first you are afraid that the other you will want you to leave, but you soon find that the two of you are the same in every way—and that includes enjoying being a twin! The other you shares everything with you, just the way *you* would, though you can't help but feel that it's *you* who is doing the sharing.

The next day the two of you set out with your new family on a trip to Moropa, just across the Paclantic Sea, on a planet like earth in another universe, that is almost, but not quite, exactly like your own.

The End

Walking toward you is a man wearing sneakers, blue jeans, and a dark blue sweater. His brownish gray hair is rumpled and he looks a bit older than your father. As he approaches, you can't see anything *strange* about him.

"Who is he?" you ask. "And what's so strange about him?"

The woman looks at you intently. "He is Edward Packard, an author who writes Choose Your Own Adventure® books."

"You've got to be kidding!"

"She's not kidding," says Packard, who has come close enough to overhear you. Holding out a hand, he says, "Glad to meet you."

You shake hands and introduce yourself. Then you realize the absurdity of the situation.

"Tell me," you demand, "how can *you* be here?"

"It's really not that surprising," he replies. "Anything can happen in hyperspace."

You think a moment, and then say, "Well, since you're the author, you ought to be able to tell me how to get *out* of hyperspace and back to my own universe!"

Suddenly the ground shakes as if an earthquake were beginning. "Cracks will appear around us soon," says Packard. "You'll have to do everything you can to avoid them!"

Go on to the next page.

Sure enough, cracks begin to open up around you. You scramble to avoid falling in. The ground rumbles like thunder. For some reason, none of the cracks are opening up around Packard. He seems perfectly safe.

"Is there a choice soon?" you ask. You're almost out of breath. "Oh, yes," Packard yells, for by now he has to shout to be heard. "Here's the choice: *Do you decide to jump into a big crack, or try to keep from falling in?*"

"Jump? Are you crazy?" you yell back.

"It might be the only way of getting out of here," Packard answers.

"What do you mean *might*?" you cry. "Tell me the right choice!"

Turn to page 86.

Convinced that the bottle can't *really* contain hyperspace, you decide to unscrew the cap. You count each turn until, after fourteen turns, the cap comes off, just as the professor had said. You hold the bottle upright at arm's length. Nothing happens, and you begin to laugh. Your laugh becomes a gasp when you begin to rise rapidly through the air. There's not far to go. *THUNK!* Your head smashes into the ceiling, knocking you out cold.

Turn to page 87.

"What *are* they?" You look at Dr. Vivaldi for help. But her face is taut, her voice grim. "Invaders from the Arcturus system. I never thought they'd get here so soon. Quick, into the space boat!" She opens the door of an egg-shaped, silver astrocraft waiting nearby. You hadn't noticed it before.

"Where did *that* come from?" you say.

Dr. Vivaldi's voice is impatient. "The author provided it so we'd have a chance to fight off the invaders. Quick!"

"Huh?"

"Hurry!" she cries. "They're almost within range!"

You hesitate. It's so bizarre. Can hyperspace really change fact into fiction?

Dr. Vivaldi is already aboard the astrocraft. A steady electronic hum tells you she has commenced countdown.

"I have no choice," she shouts. "But *you* do, and you've got to make it *now.*"

If you board the astrocraft and prepare for takeoff, turn to page 110.

If you decide that, since this is just a book, it's not worth bothering to climb aboard, turn to page 90.

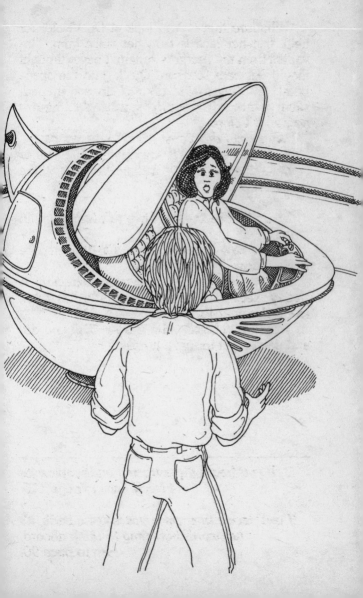

You're flying! You're tiny. You can't see that you're tiny. You just *feel* that way. You stretch your arms and feel your ribbed wings stretch. Electronic sounds wail in your ears, rising and falling in pitch. *You* are making them!

Instinctively you stretch your wings and tilt them up and then down. In an instant you lose speed, flip your body, and dig the claws of your tiny hind legs into the rough bark of a tree.

Hanging upside down. Sniffing for insects. Forming a sound picture of the grove of trees in which you've alighted: the big rocks, a fat bird pecking. Your sonar organ clicks at superhigh frequency . . . .

No time to think much—you're hungry! Flying. *Zrrrrbeeeee.* Homing in on a large, meaty fly. Snap. Snap. Munch.

Now you listen again to your sonar *click, clk, clik, clk* . . . as you search for the cool, damp cave that is your home.

The End

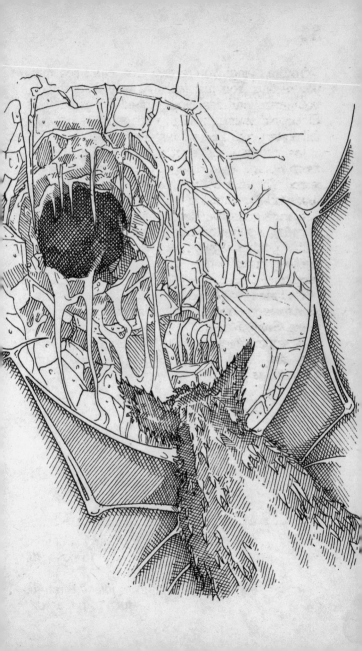

Packard starts to answer, but suddenly a great crack opens up under him. *"AAIEEE!"* he cries as he disappears into the abyss.

You look around for the woman, but she is gone. You are all alone.

*If you jump into one of the big cracks,
turn to page 95.*

*If you try to keep from falling through,
turn to page 102.*

An hour or so later you come to with a bad headache. Good grief, you're lying on the *ceiling*! Your head still hurts, and you lapse back into unconsciousness. When you next awaken, you're drifting slowly toward the floor. A few minutes later you touch down, but you feel strangely light—as if you weighed only a few pounds.

It's several hours before you return to your normal weight. You're grateful to have survived your encounter with hyperspace, and thankful you weren't outdoors when you opened the professor's bottle. If you had been, you'd be passing the moon by now.

The End

You have your doubts about whether or not the bottle really contains hyperspace, but there's nothing to lose by saving it.

Nearly six months have passed when you see a newspaper headline that almost knocks you off your feet.

PROFESSOR'S DISCOVERY FATAL

While a group of stunned scientists from the National Research Institute watched in horror, Professor Karl Zinka opened a bottle allegedly filled with hyperspace and was immediately flung into the stratosphere. He was tracked by radar, but contact was lost at the 80,000-foot level. It is not believed that he could have survived. . . .

Turn to page 94.

You follow the others, trying to stay in the dream. The doctor turns around. "Get back in bed. You can't come into the operating room!"

You glare at him. He glares back. "Nurse, I think this patient needs a sedative."

The nurse starts toward you. In her hand is a large hypodermic needle. Now you're getting angry. They can't do this to you—not even if you're just somebody in somebody else's dream!

Turn to page 93.

"I want to control my own life," you tell Dr. Vivaldi. "I just don't want to do what some author tells me to. I want . . ."

"I understand." Dr. Vivaldi waves at you as the door to the astrocraft slides shut. A moment later her craft is airborne. You stand watching, hoping she will be able to outmaneuver the invaders.

If Dr. Vivaldi is right, hyperspace has somehow reduced you to being a mere character in a book. What a dilemma! What can you do about it?

In a flash the answer comes. You stop reading!

The End

You wake up stretched out on the floor of a laboratory similar to Dr. Zinka's. Three men in white coats are looking down at you.

One of them leans over and helps you to your feet. "I'm sorry our guard was so rough with you," he says. "In Primo universe we have a strict policy about aliens."

"I'm an alien?"

"Yes, in the most profound sense. Although you look as human as we do and live in a country almost identical to ours, you are from another universe, and so we must expel you."

"What do you mean?"

"Please step onto that white disc painted on the floor."

You argue for a moment; then, realizing that you have no choice, you take the step. In the next instant you are jettisoned into hyperspace.

Turn to page 100.

That night you sleep fitfully and wake before dawn. No one else is up, and you lie in bed trying to remember who you are. Maybe you should walk back to the spot in the park where you first woke up, or maybe it would be better just to wait for your meeting with the hypnotist.

If you walk back to the park, turn to page 96.

If you wait for your appointment, turn to page 109.

Suddenly you understand in a flash. You're not in just any dream; *you* are the one who is dreaming! The doctor, the nurse, and the patient exist only in *your* imagination!

The doctor must know it too; he begins to fade out of your dream.

"I'm not really sick!" the patient cries.

"You're not really real!" the nurse corrects him, as you wake up smiling.

The End

After reading the article, you take out your own bottle of hyperspace and gaze at it with new respect.

Three days later a group of scientists from the National Institute pay a call on you. The leader of the delegation, Dr. Wolsetter, tells you that Dr. Zinka's papers revealed that you own the only other bottle of hyperspace in existence.

"First of all," says Dr. Wolsetter, "we must warn you not to open the bottle."

"You don't need to tell me," you reply. "I'm not taking any chances."

"I didn't think you would," says Dr. Wolsetter. "We would like to study the hyperspace in your bottle. It could be of enormous benefit to mankind. But the bottle must only be opened under carefully controlled laboratory conditions. We are authorized to pay you for it."

"How much?" you ask.

Dr. Wolsetter smiles. "I'm afraid we can offer you only a tiny fraction of its true worth."

"Okay, but how much?"

"One million dollars."

One million dollars! That's a lot of money. You almost blurt out, "I'll take it." But then you stop for a moment to wonder. How much is a bottle of hyperspace worth? "I'll think it over and let you know tomorrow," you answer.

The scientists bid you good night, saying that they will call on you again in the morning. You have trouble sleeping that night, but you don't mind one bit.

The End

You decide to jump into one of the big cracks.

It occurs to you that Packard must have been able to survive, or he wouldn't have been able to write the book *Hyperspace*. You stare into one of the bottomless cracks opening almost beneath your feet. It hardly seems to offer much hope, but sometimes you just have to make a leap of faith.

But the moment you jump, you regret it. Clouds of white vapor rise up all around you as you fall. There's no way of telling how far you'll fall, and, judging by the speed at which the clouds rush past, you're accelerating at a tremendous rate. It's as if you were falling toward a planet with gravity far stronger than the earth's!

Then you see a human form hurtling through the mists beneath you—Packard!

"Will I make it?" you shout.

"Sorry, but I can't remember how this ends," he yells back.

You start to answer, but a cloud of vapor engulfs you. You barely have strength enough to breathe.

Turn to page 116.

When you reach the park, you're amazed to see someone sitting on a bench—someone who looks exactly like you!

You're almost reluctant to meet someone who looks so much like yourself. On the other hand, you're curious. But you don't have long to think about it. Your double runs toward you, calling, "I'm glad you came back! Professor Zinka is in his lab in your old universe, ready to activate the hypolaser and bring me back there. You can come too if you want."

"Who are *you*, and who is Professor Zinka?" you ask.

Turn to page 99.

"I don't understand this at all," you say, "but I know that I want to get back to the universe where I started out—so I'll come along."

The other you starts to reply, but at that moment you feel a terrific jolt . . . .

Turn to page 103.

You decide to stay where you are.

Shaking your head, you step aside from the contact point. "Good luck."

The other you nods. "And to *you.*"

An instant later you are alone. You head back to Dr. Firenze's house. It looks as if hypnosis is your only hope of getting your memory back. As you walk along the road you see a man whose face seems vaguely familiar. Somehow you know that his name is Professor Zinka. How can this be? Professor Zinka just contacted the other you from another universe! But no, it must be . . . he's coming toward you.

Turn to page 105.

"I'm the other you, of course," is the reply. "What's the matter with you?"

"Well, as a matter of fact, I don't know. My memory of my life is only one day long."

The other you looks at you closely. "Then you don't know."

"Know what?"

"The professor has determined that when we traveled through hyperspace our identities were scrambled."

"What do you mean?"

The other you looks you in the eye. "The problem is that now you're *me.*"

"Huh?"

"And I'm *you!* I remember everything that ever happened to you. My body's identical to yours. If you hadn't just lost your memory, you would have all the memories of my life. The truth is that it's my memory you've lost, not yours."

"What can we do about this?" you start to ask, when suddenly your hair stands on end and your body tingles from head to toe.

Turn to page 104.

Seconds later you have a piercing vision—a vision so intense that your mind can't retain it. You have no idea how long you remain in this state, since you know that in hyperspace time may move faster or slower than in our familiar world.

When the vision passes, you are sure that you are not just a figure in someone's dream or a character in a book. You are a real flesh and blood person! And all you know about hyperspace is in the book you're holding.

As you open it, your eyes rest on page 3.

Turn to page 3.

As you start explaining, the boy runs up to join you and Susan. "This is my brother Pete," she says.

They listen attentively to your story. "You'd better come home with us," says Susan. "Our father is a doctor."

"Yeah, he'll fix you up," Pete adds.

An hour later you're in the examining room of Dr. Howard Reid. He looks into your eyes with an ophthalmoscope. He makes you touch your nose with one eye closed. He asks you lots of questions. Finally he leans back in his chair and looks at you curiously.

"I'm afraid you have acute amnesia," he says. "You may have knocked your head—though I can't detect any injury—or you may have had an emotional shock that made you repress everything you knew about yourself. My nurse has already checked with the police, and no one of your description has been reported missing. You can stay with our family awhile, but tomorrow I want you to see my colleague, Dr. Firenze. He will hypnotize you; then perhaps you'll remember who you are."

Turn to page 92.

It just doesn't make sense to jump into the cracks. Even Packard didn't jump—he *fell* in!

So you keep scrambling and jumping around, hoping the earthquake or whatever it is will soon be over. But the whole land surface is bouncing as if it were an enormous bedspread being shaken by giants.

WHOOSH! Suddenly you're rising so fast it's as if you had become a rocket. Clouds swirl around you. Quivering lights shine from different angles. The clouds are shining reds, blues, yellows, and colors you've never seen in your life!

Some special cosmic knowledge must have entered your brain, for somehow you know what's happening: you're crossing into the *sixth* dimension—the first human being ever to do so . . . .

Turn to page 106.

The professor must have found your coordinates, because here you are, reading this book. Apparently you are back in your own universe, and you *are* you.

Best of all, your memory seems normal again. In fact, everything seems okay, except—suppose that, instead of being yourself, you're really the *other* you. It's just possible, and in that case you might never know it, for the other you may have the same memories you have.

There's just no way of being sure that the *you* you were is the *you* you are now.

The End

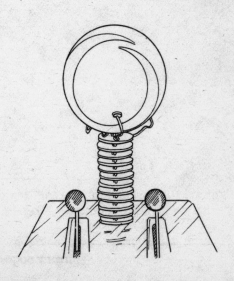

"Uh-oh," says the other you. "The professor has found your coordinates. He's ready to activate the switch and bring us back. You have only a moment to decide."

"Decide what?"

"Why, whether to go with me or stay. I would think you'd rather stay. After all, now that you're me, this is *your* planet in *your* universe. Actually, as long as you've lost your memory, it doesn't make much difference where you are, so long as it's a nice place to live. But if you do get your memory back, you'll be glad you're here with my—I mean with *your* own family and friends."

You're confused, but there's not much time to think.

If you say that you'll go along with the other you, turn to page 97.

If you decide to stay where you are, turn to page 98.

"There you are!" he cries. "I felt so badly that you'd lost your memory."

"Professor Zinka? I thought you were in another universe!"

The professor smiles. "That's the other Professor Zinka. I'm right here in *this* universe. And one thing that's different in this universe is that I'm more competent than the other Professor Zinka. So follow me back to my laboratory. I'm going to get you back to your own home in your own universe with your own memory."

"Thanks, Professor," you say. "I don't know if you know it or not, but the other me went back there already because he thought our identities had been switched."

"No, no, no!" The professor pats you on the back. "It was the *other* Professor Zinka and I whose identities were switched." He gives you another pat on the back. "I'm not sure of much, my young friend, but I *am* sure of this: *You definitely are YOU!*—At least I hope so."

The End

[Unfortunately, the author of this book, Edward Packard, never made it to the sixth dimension. For that reason he is unable to describe it. Maybe you can, or maybe it can never be described at all.]

The End

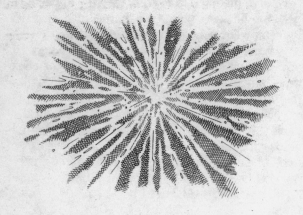

"Nera Vivaldi! I know who you are. You're a character in some books I've read: *Third Planet from Altair, Survival at Sea,* and *Underground Kingdom!"*

"I'm the one," she replies, "and now, of course, I'm a character in *Hyperspace.* Like Professor Zinka, I've been working to develop a device that would penetrate hyperspace. At last I succeeded, so it was only natural for me to be in this book!"

"But we're not in a book—this is *real.* I *really* exist," you say nervously, "and so do you!"

Turn to page 111.

Later that morning you're sitting in the consulting room of Dr. Guido Firenze, psychiatrist and hypnotist.

"Just keep your eyes on the light swinging from the chain." The doctor speaks in a kind but monotonous tone. "You're beginning to feel sleepy, very sleepy . . . ."

Slowly you close your eyes and think. Slowly you begin to remember. It's coming back to you. You were born on the planet Zog, and pulling the red lever must have caused you to switch identities with a creature that's rare even on Zog. This creature begins life in the form of a human being. At the age of sixteen it spins a cocoon around itself. About three months later it emerges as the furry-haired gurumba, a Zogian animal that looks very much like an Abyssinian cat.

The End

You jump aboard. The door slides shut. Dr. Vivaldi turns a knob and pulls a lever. The craft rises silently into the air. You monitor its ascent on the display readout. You're confident that her astrocraft has an advanced design, capable of meeting any challenge.

"Look!" Dr. Vivaldi points to the display screen. "The incoming fleet is accelerating."

Scores of tiny images appear on the screen, dancing like a swarm of bees.

You look anxiously at Dr. Vivaldi. A buzzer sounds. Warning lights flash. She works furiously at the instrument panel. "I'm trying to get us into evasive escape mode."

Turn to page 114.

Dr. Vivaldi smiles and shakes her head. "I wish I could exist in reality. I think I could make quite a contribution to the world, but unfortunately that isn't my destiny. I was fated to be nothing more than a character in a book, and that's all I ever shall be."

"Maybe so," you reply grudgingly. "But I *am* real. I want to get out of this hospital and maybe even out of this universe!"

Your tone is so angry that you're afraid Dr. Vivaldi may be offended; instead she laughs pleasantly. "I know how you feel, and I'm sorry to tell you that you too are only a fictional character. We're both in the same boat, both in the same book!"

"I can understand that *you're* just a character, but how did this happen to *me*?"

"It happened," she says gently, "because you entered hyperspace, where things are neither what they seem nor even what we imagined they would be."

You feel so frustrated you could cry. Being a character in a book is no better than being a character in someone's dream!

Turn to page 115.

You look up from the book. It might be worth reading it some more. On the other hand, maybe you should go back to the professor's house and see what he's up to.

If you decide to spend some more time reading the book, go on to the next page.

If you go back and talk to the professor himself, turn to page 6.

You start to reread the professor's book, trying to understand his strange ideas.

> *Imagine that you are absolutely flat, you read, and that you live on a flat surface. You can travel backward and forward and sideways, but never up and down. In fact, you never even know there is an up and down!*
>
> *Of course in the real world you can move backward and forward AND up and down. But imagine still another way you could travel—a way we cannot even describe. If you could move in THAT direction, you'd be in hyperspace!*

The words make a little more sense this time, and you decide to read further without skipping ahead.

Turn to page 4.

The enemy craft close in. They're coming at you from all directions. Dr. Vivaldi wipes her perspiring brow. Then she sits motionless, the blood drained from her face. "It's no use. They are a very advanced life form. We have only a few seconds to live."

You start to scream, but she leans over and punches your arm. "It's only a *book*. We'll have another chance. . . ."

The End

"Don't be sad," Dr. Vivaldi says. "Come, follow me. I've got something to show you."

Dr. Vivaldi has always been a nice person in the books you've read, but now she seems to be acting very strangely. If anything, she's making your problems worse. Should you go with her or try to get out of this on your own?

If you go with Dr. Vivaldi, turn to page 74.

If you tell her "no, thanks" and set out on your own, turn to page 75.

You're still alive. You can wiggle your toes and blink your eyes! You're on the planet earth, but you feel as if you have arrived here for the first time. You can see everything more clearly now. You notice the colors, the shades of light, the sounds of voices, human faces; you take in the excitement, boredom, pleasure, worry, and joy of everyone around you. And you see the sky, the trees, the angles and lines made by familiar objects; you notice the sunlight, a plane droning overhead; you feel the cool breeze blowing.

It's good to be back in your own universe. After all, it's home.

The End

ABOUT THE AUTHOR

EDWARD PACKARD is a graduate of Princeton University and Columbia Law School. He developed the unique storytelling approach used in the Choose Your Own Adventure® series while thinking up stories for his children, Caroline, Andrea, and Wells.

ABOUT THE ILLUSTRATOR

ANTHONY KRAMER graduated from the Paier School of Art in Hamden, Connecticut, where he received the Children's Book Illustration award. He has been an editorial cartoonist, an architectural artist, and a designer of children's-toy packages. His illustrated books for children include *Underground Kingdom* by Edward Packard and *Secret of the Pyramids* by Richard Brightfield, both for Bantam's Choose Your Own Adventure® series. Mr. Kramer lives in New York City where he loves to walk, run, and bicycle.

DO YOU LOVE CHOOSE YOUR OWN ADVENTURE®?

Let your younger brothers and sisters in on the fun.

You know how great CHOOSE YOUR OWN ADVENTURE® books are to read and reread. But did you know that there are CHOOSE YOUR OWN ADVENTURE® books for younger kids too? They're just as thrilling as the CHOOSE YOUR OWN ADVENTURE® books you read and they're filled with the same kinds of decisions and different ways for the stories to end— but they're shorter with more illustrations and come in a larger, easier-to-read size.

So get your younger brothers and sisters and anyone else you know between the ages of seven and nine in on the fun by introducing them to the exciting world of CHOOSE YOUR OWN ADVENTURE®.

Bantam CHOOSE YOUR OWN ADVENTURE® books for younger readers, on sale wherever paperbacks are sold:

#1 THE CIRCUS by Edward Packard
#2 THE HAUNTED HOUSE by R. A. Montgomery
#3 SUNKEN TREASURE by Edward Packard
#4 YOUR VERY OWN ROBOT by R. A. Montgomery
#5 GORGA, THE SPACE MONSTER by Edward Packard
#6 THE GREEN SLIME by R. A. Montgomery
#7 HELP! YOU'RE SHRINKING by Edward Packard
#8 INDIAN TRAIL by R. A. Montgomery

AV7—4/83